My first picture book for my first

grandchild—Brevin Michael Warrick

—K. C. W.

In memory of Jennifer M. Darr,

a childhood friend, 1956–1968

—S. N.

The illustrations were rendered in gouache and colored pencil
The text type was set in BernhardMod BT
The display type was set in BernhardMod Bd BT
Composed in the United States of America
Designed by Lois A. Rainwater
Edited by Aimee Jackson
Production supervised by Lisa Brownfield

Printed in Hong Kong by Wing King Tong Company Limited

FIRST IMPRESSION
ISBN 0-87358-781-2

Warrick, Karen Clemens
If I had a tail / Karen Clemens Warrick;
illustrated by Sherry Neidigh.
p.   cm.
Summary: The reader is asked to guess what a creature
is from a description of the appearance and use of its tail.
ISBN 0-87358-781-2 (alk. paper)
[1. Tail—Fiction. 2. Animals—Fiction.] I. Neidigh, Sherry, ill. II. Title.

PZ7.W2576 Iae 2001
[E]—dc21   00-051007

296/7.5M/3–01

If I Had a Tail

by KAREN CLEMENS WARRICK

illustrated by SHERRY NEIDIGH

rising moon

If I had a tail,

a tail like a log afloat,

a gray-green tail to help me swim,

I would snap my tail like a cracking whip.

I'd be an…

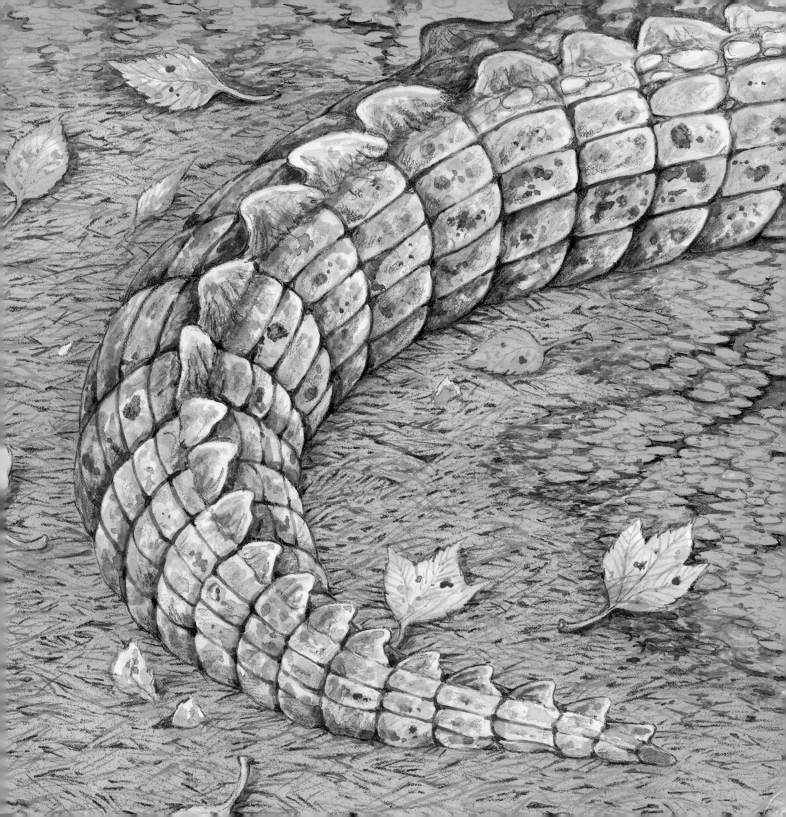

Alligator

If I had a tail,

a tail like a snuggly slipper,

a beautiful, bushy black-and-white tail,

then I could scare a grizzly bear.

I'd be a…

Skunk

If I had a tail,

a tail like a

day-old pancake,

a brown, scaly tail shaped like my bill,

then I could duck down under water.

I'd be a...

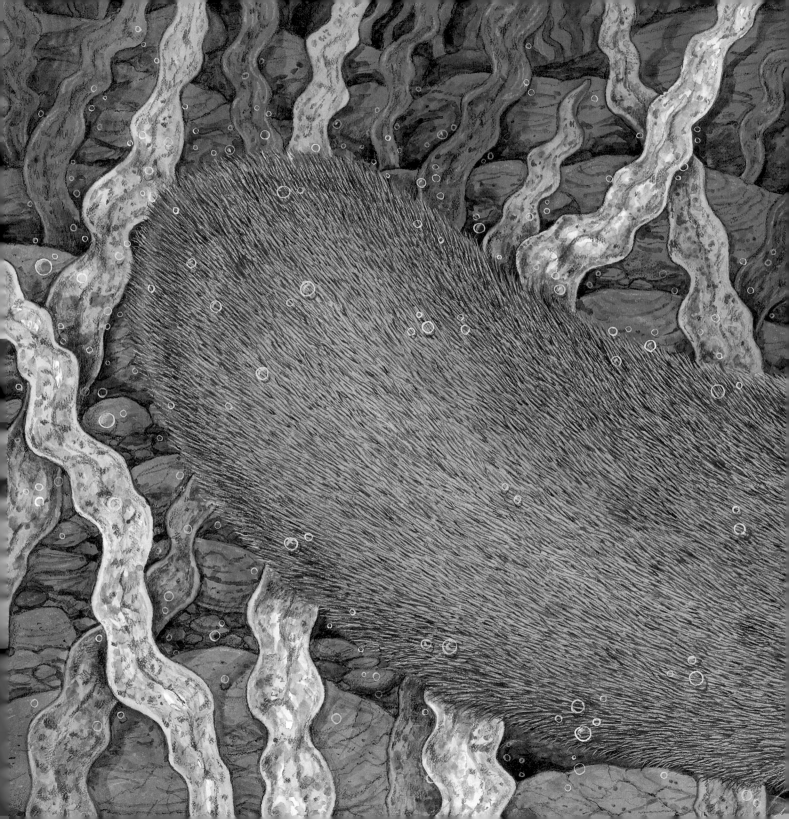

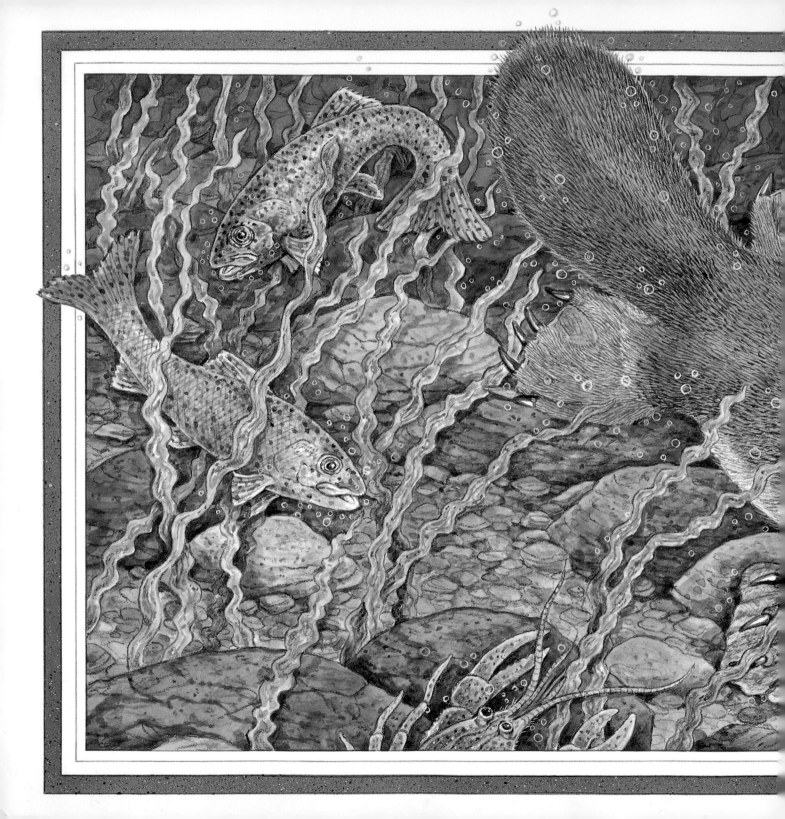

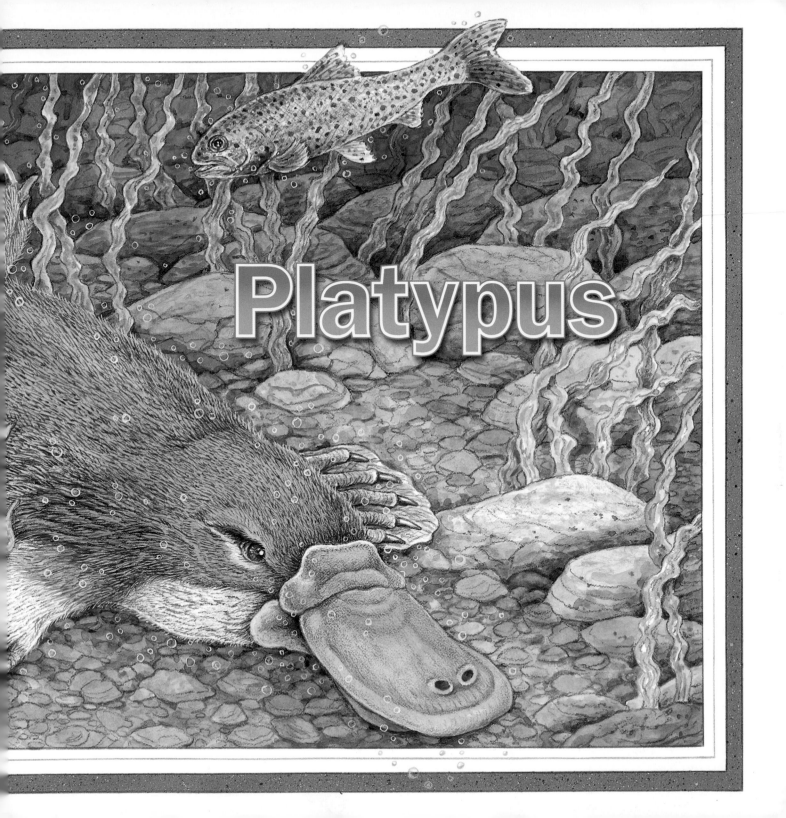

Platypus

If I had a tail,

a tail like a green, speckled whip,

so brittle it breaks

when grabbed by a hawk,

then I'd scurry away to grow a new tail.

I'd be a…

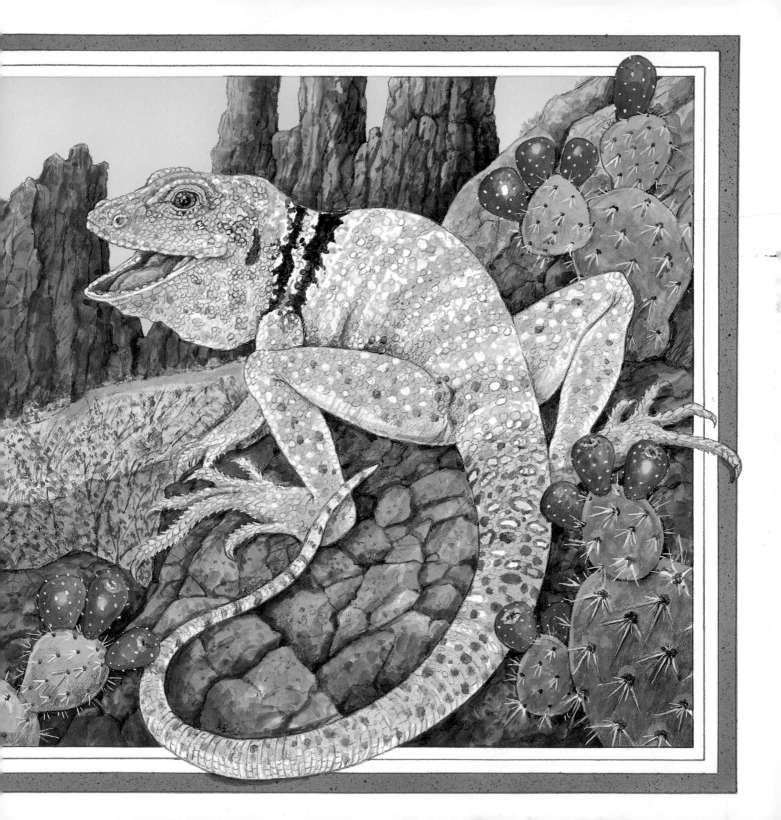

If I had a tail,

a tail that gripped

like a hand,

then I could go

down a tree—nose first,

or take a rest with my head hanging low.

I'd be an…

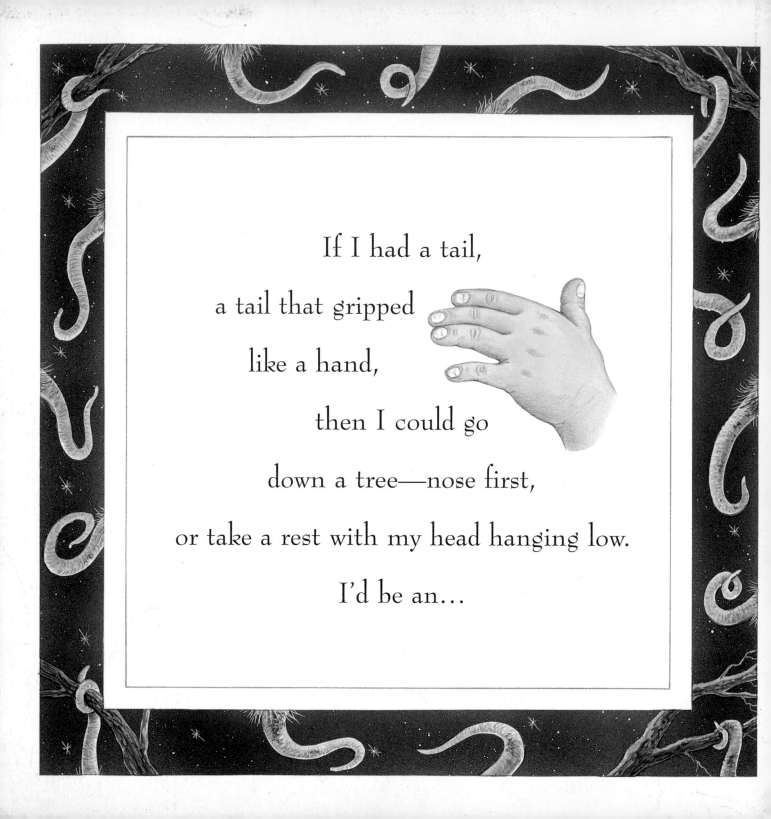

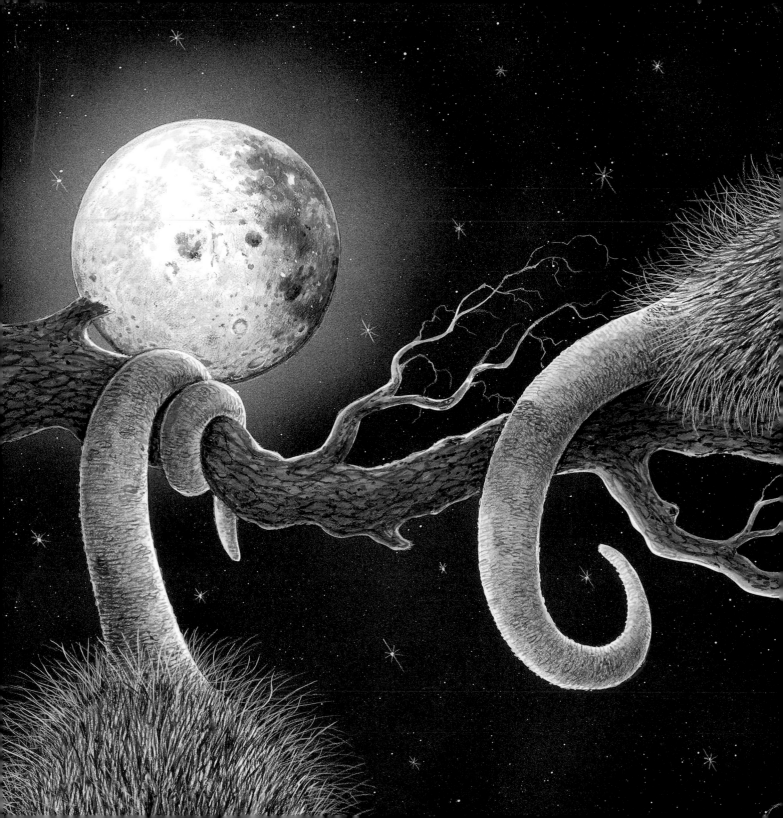

Opossum

If I had a tail,

a tail like

a colorful fan,

with plumes that unfold

to glitter and shimmer,

sprinkled with eyes

watching you watching me,

I'd be a…

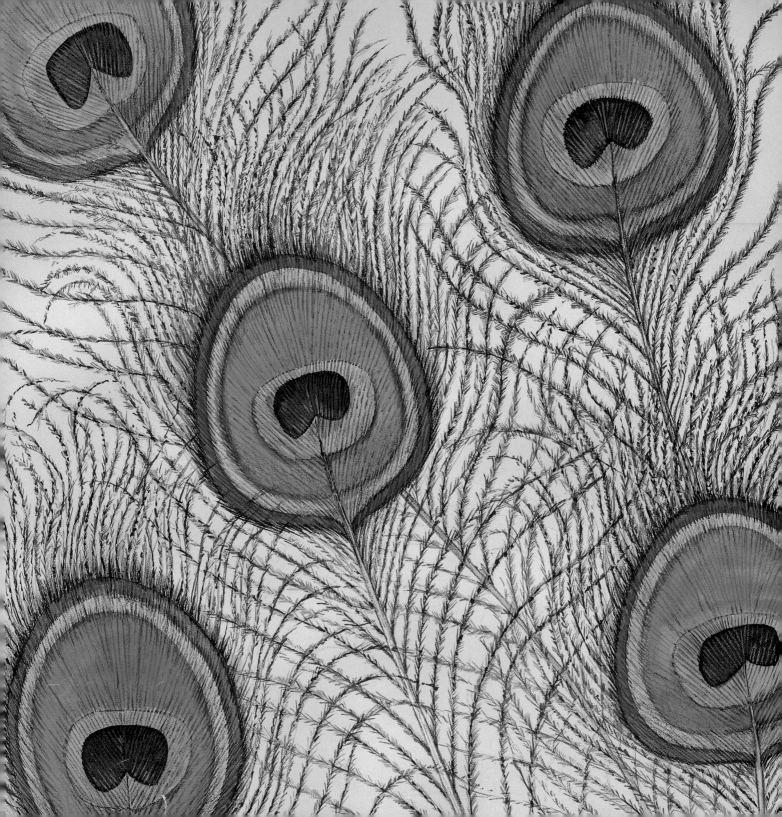

Peacock

If I had a tail,

a tail tough as armor,

a wrap-around tail

with bumpy, sharp spines,

then I'd tie up to coral

as dinner drifts by.

I'd be a…

Sea horse

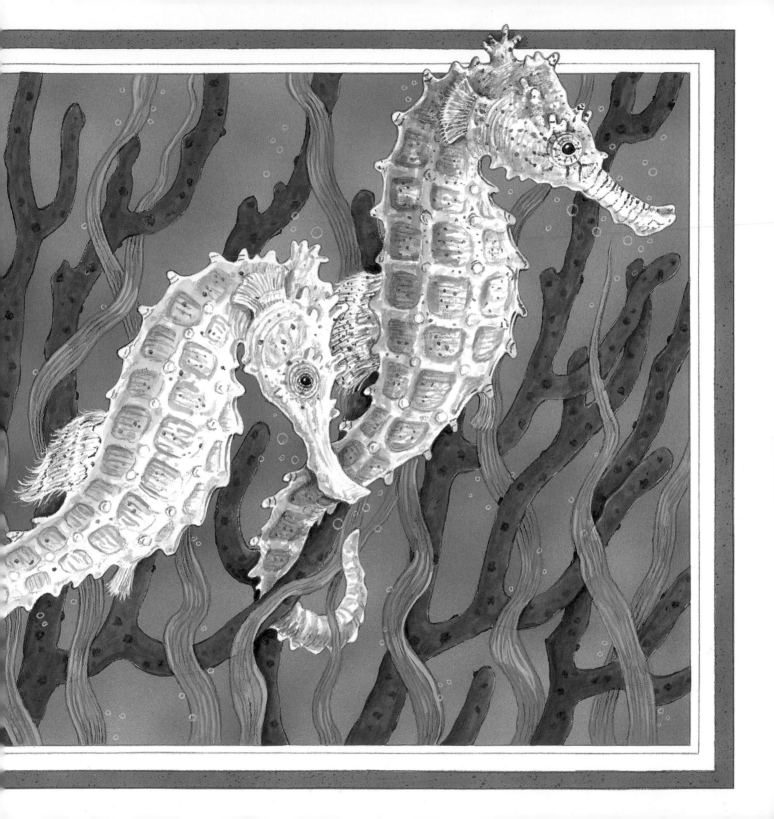

Now you take a turn
and imagine a tail.

Just begin with these words:

If I had a tail…

KAREN CLEMENS WARRICK is a freelance writer and former elementary school teacher of fifteen years. She has written student integrated science units, articles for teacher publications, and has published three young-adult biographies.

When she is not writing, she loves to travel and explore new places while hiking, biking, and snow skiing. Karen lives in Prescott, Arizona, with her husband and two dogs.

SHERRY NEIDIGH has been an artist nearly all her life. She began drawing at the age of two and has been illustrating professionally for the past fifteen years. She has illustrated numerous books, including *Creatures at My Feet* and *Black and White,* both by Rising Moon.

Sherry lives in Charlotte, North Carolina, with her two sheltie dogs, Basil Knawbone and Chloe.